The
Bollo
Caper

From:
Kandy Brown
1974

The Bollo Caper

A fable for children of all ages

Art Buchwald

Illustrated by Julie Brinckloe

Doubleday & Company, Inc.
Garden City, New York

ISBN: *0-385-01025-7 Trade*
     0-385-03185-8 Prebound
Library of Congress Catalog Card Number 73–10857
Copyright © 1973, 1974 by Art Buchwald
All Rights Reserved
Printed in the United States of America
First Edition

The
Bollo
Caper

F ELIX THE FURRIER WAS FITTING AN Alaskan seal coat on the very wealthy Mrs. Boomala Van Carcus, when his secretary burst into the fitting room and said breathlessly,

"Lulu La Looche, the famous and glamorous movie star, is calling you from Beverly Hills, California, and says she must talk to you immediately."

"Drat that woman," said Felix the Furrier. "She drives me up the wall."

The secretary said, "She says it is a matter of life and death."

Felix threw his tape measure down in disgust and went to the telephone on the wall.

"Lulu, sweetheart," he said. "What a pleasant surprise to hear from you."

"Dahling Felix," Lulu said. "I am so depressed, I had to talk to you."

"Tell your Felix everything, my little Lulu."

Lulu sniffled on the phone, "I don't have a fur coat to wear to the Oscar Awards dinner."

"How can you say that?" Felix said. "I sold you five minks, three sables, one chinchilla, and a floor-length silver fox."

"They are so boring." Lulu said. "Everyone has seen me in them. I want something new, something fantastic, something that will make Hollywood stand on its ear."

"That's a tough order," Felix the Furrier said.

"Felix, as you know, my sixth husband is the fourth richest man in the world and he said he didn't care what it cost as long as I was happy. Money is no object, Felix, but you must find me the perfect fur coat or I will die."

"Don't die, Lulu. Your Uncle Felix will come up with something if it kills me."

"Dahling, my life is in your hands."

After Felix the Furrier hung up he ordered one of his assistants to finish fitting the very wealthy Mrs. Boomala Van Carcus and went into his office to place a long-distance call to the Carstair brothers in Nairobi, Kenya.

The Carstair brothers were the most famous hunters of rare furs in all of Africa, and Felix knew if anyone was able to find the right pelt for a new coat for Lulu La Looche, they could.

When Felix explained the problem, the Carstair brothers became very excited.

"We have heard of a fantastic Somali leopard who lives in the jungle of northern Ethiopia," one of the Carstair brothers said. "The natives call him Bollo and he is supposed to have the most beautiful skin of any leopard on the continent. It is tawny yellow with bright black spots so evenly distributed on his body that you might have thought someone printed them on him by hand."

"The reason we haven't ever tried to catch him," the other Carstair brother said, "is that it would cost fifteen thousand dollars to organize an expedition to find him."

"Don't worry about the cost," Felix the Furrier said. "I want that leopard. And catch him alive because I plan to get a fantastic amount of publicity out of it."

"Alive?" said a Carstair brother. "Alive will cost you another ten thousand dollars, not counting the shipping and insurance."

"I told you," Felix shouted over the telephone, "I don't care how much I have to pay. Get me the leopard."

A few months later, Bollo, the most beautiful male leopard in all of Africa, was strolling on his way to meet with his girl friend, the seductive and curvaceous Nefertiti, the most beautiful *female* leopard in all of Africa. It was Bollo's custom after a delicious dinner to seek out Nefertiti and cuddle up with her on a pile of banana leaves, licking her nose and ears.

Jungle gossip had it that Bollo and Nefertiti, who had been seeing each other for two years, were soon going to get married. But Bollo always maintained that he wasn't ready to settle down and have a family. This annoyed Nefertiti no end because, after two

years, a female leopard likes to have a little security.

In any case, Bollo found Nefertiti in their favorite spot and stretched out beside her. He started nuzzling her back, which he knew gave Nefertiti great pleasure, when suddenly they heard the sound of native drums beating a fast "boom," "boom," "boom."

Bollo jumped up. Behind him he heard other natives screaming war chants. He said to Nefertiti, "I don't like the smell of this. Go up to the top of the tree and hide."

"What will you do?" Nefertiti cried.

"I'll get them away from here," Bollo said.

"I'm afraid for you," Nefertiti said, clutching his neck.

"Don't worry," said Bollo. "They can't catch me. Now hurry, up the tree. And stay there until I come back."

Nefertiti looked back once and then climbed up to the top branches of the tree. The drums and native cries kept coming closer and closer.

Bollo crouched and waited. Finally the

natives broke through a clearing and Bollo, making sure they saw him, started to run down a path he knew very well. What he could not have known was this was exactly what the Carstair brothers counted on. Bollo was so intent on getting away from the natives, he did not notice a large hole that had been dug in the path until the last moment. He tried to leap it, but it was too much of a jump and Bollo plummeted down, down, down into a large net in the bottom of the hole.

Bollo fought like a tiger to get out, but the more he struggled, the tighter the net became, until he was hopelessly trapped, unable to move.

Suddenly a bright light lit up the hole and Bollo heard a voice shout, "We got him. We got him."

The other voice said, "Oh boy, look at that skin. Felix the Furrier is going to go ape when he sees him."

The first voice said, "Give me the tranquilizer gun and we will put him to sleep."

Bollo, who was blinded by the light, could not see what was going on, but as he

lay dazed in the net he heard a bang and immediately felt a sharp stab in his beautiful tawny bottom. In a few minutes he yawned once, then twice. Try as he could, he was unable to stay awake. As he dozed off into a dreamless sleep, the last words he heard from the top of the hole were, "We'll put him on the first plane to New York."

Bollo did not know how long he was asleep, but when he woke up he found himself in a small wooden crate suffering from a terrible headache. As his eyes got accustomed to the dark, he was able to make out another crate with two chimpanzees in it.

"Where am I?" Bollo croaked.

"You're on a special animal cargo jet airplane," one of the chimpanzees said, "on the way to the United States of America. We thought you'd never wake up."

The other chimpanzee said, "Bollo, I want you to know it's an honor for us to be on the same airplane with you. We heard at the airport that you're being taken to America to become a fur coat for the famous movie star Lulu La Looche."

"A fur coat?" Bollo said. "You've got to be kidding."

"I'm not joking," the chimpanzee replied. "They said you had one of the most beautiful skins of any animal in Africa and in less than a month you would be draping the lovely curves of Lulu La Looche."

"But I don't want to be a fur coat," Bollo protested.

"The choice isn't yours," the chimpanzee said. "We don't want to be in the space program, but that's what they're bringing us back for."

The other chimpanzee said, "They're going to shoot us off in rockets, and we both have a fear of heights."

Bollo was starting to get angry. "Well, I have news for both of you. No one is going to make me into a fur coat for a stupid movie star."

"I wish you luck," the chimpanzee said.

"Who else is on the plane?" Bollo asked.

"There are several monkeys who are going to be part of a cancer research project, a lion going to the Bronx Zoo, and twenty snakes who, we understand, are going to become shoes to go with Lulu La Looche's fur coat, which happens to be you."

As they were talking, the pilot's voice came over the loudspeaker.

"We are entering a patch of very bumpy air and I would advise you all to fasten your seat belts. Also, please refrain from smoking."

Even before the pilot had finished his announcement, the plane took a bounce, then a dive, then another bounce and it shuddered. The crates went flying all over the cabin. Bollo's crate hit the side of the plane, then it went skidding into the chimpanzees' crate, then it turned over on its side.

The animals were screaming and yelling. For twenty minutes, the plane zigzagged crazily through the sky. Bollo, who wasn't feeling too good to start with, got airsick and threw up.

Finally, the plane quieted down and was sailing along smoothly again. The pilot turned off the FASTEN YOUR SEAT BELT sign. Bollo, dazed by the bumpy ride and embarrassed by getting sick, pushed the side of the crate and discovered, to his surprise, it fell off. Apparently the rough trip had loosened the boards.

All of a sudden, Bollo was outside in the cabin of the plane.

The chimpanzees were chattering excitedly. "You'd better get back in your crate, Bollo, or they're going to get very mad."

"Not me," Bollo replied. "As soon as we land, I'm going to make a break for it."

"Don't do it," one of the chimpanzees begged. "You'll never get away. They'll shoot you dead."

Bollo said, "Either way they'll shoot me dead. This way, at least I've got a chance. Do you guys want to make the break with me?"

"No, thanks," one of the chimpanzees replied. "Going up in a space capsule might not be much, but it's better than winding up in a coffin at Kennedy Airport."

The plane landed at the airport at ten o'clock at night. Unbeknown to the animals on board, Felix the Furrier had told all the newspapers and television stations in New York City that Lulu La Looche's fur coat was arriving at Gate No. 25.

The cameramen and reporters with floodlights blazing waited impatiently for the doors of the jet airplane to open.

Bollo peered out of one of the tiny windows to size up the situation. There were armed guards everywhere. This was going to be more difficult than he thought.

Then he got an idea. With his two front paws, he replaced the side of the crate and pushed the nails back into their holes. Then he went to the bathroom in the back of the plane and locked it. He sat down on the toilet seat and waited.

Stairs were wheeled up to the plane and an armed guard opened up the cabin door.

The reporters and cameramen pressed forward.

"Wait," said Felix the Furrier. "Let them unload all the other animals first. We will save Bollo for last."

A crew of workmen started to carry off the crates of animals. No one paid any attention to the chimpanzees, or the lion, or the snakes, or the monkeys.

All they wanted was pictures of Bollo, the rare Somali leopard that was worth twenty five thousand dollars even before it had been made into a fur coat.

Finally the workers got to Bollo's crate. Two armed guards stood on each side of them because Felix said Bollo was ferocious and a man-eater. (In that way he could charge more for the coat.)

The crate did not seem very heavy to the workers, but it was too dark to look inside the box so they carried it out down the steps.

"Bring him over here," Felix the Furrier shouted. "I want to have my picture taken with him."

The workers carried the crate over to where the cameramen were waiting with their powerful lights.

"Easy does it, boys," Felix the Furrier shouted. "We don't want to do anything to damage God's gift to Lulu La Looche."

Bollo knew he only had one or two minutes. He unbolted the bathroom and padded quietly to the door and peered out. Everyone was standing around the crate. Taking the steps two at a time, he rushed down the stairs and bounded off into the darkness of

Kennedy Airport at a speed that even he didn't know he had.

As he disappeared, he heard Felix the Furrier's hysterical voice shouting,

"He's gone! He's gone! My beautiful fur coat is gone!"

"Surround the airport!" a voice yelled. *"And shoot to kill."*

Bollo ran and ran, but he didn't know where to go. He ran on the runway and two planes almost landed on him. He almost hit a fire truck but, at the last minute, jumped over it.

Then he found himself in some fields and finally he was dragging his feet in a heavily wooded swamp. It was damp and it was cold, but it seemed safe. Exhausted from all the running, not to mention the excitement, Bollo plopped down in a bed of moss and went to sleep.

That's where the three ducks found him the next morning.

"Boy, is that a big cat!" one of the ducks quacked.

Bollo woke up. He was prepared to fight. The ducks backed away.

"Don't get excited," one of the ducks said. "We're not going to hurt you. What are you doing in our swamp?"

"I'm a fugitive from a fur coat," Bollo said. "An escaped animal."

"Oh," quacked one of the ducks. "So that explains it. No wonder the helicopters have been flying around here all night long."

"And the police boats have been sounding their sirens so we couldn't sleep. We thought something was up."

"Can I get anything to eat around here?" Bollo asked. "I'm starving."

The three ducks backed away. One of them said, "Hey, wait a minute. Get that glint out of your eye."

"I didn't mean I was going to eat you," Bollo said.

"There's a garbage dump over there," one of the ducks shouted and then the three of them quickly flew away.

Bollo wandered over to the garbage dump and sniffed around. He finally found some half-eaten steaks which he eagerly munched on.

Just as he was attacking his third steak, he saw three policemen with guns beating through the reeds. Bollo began to run again. This time he found himself running along a highway which had large signs saying, TO NEW YORK. Bollo, of course, didn't know what New York was and he was tiring fast, so he decided to hitch a ride. He leaped on a yellow taxicab that was moving slowly toward the city and got a good grip on the TAXI sign on the top. Fortunately for Bollo,

his color fitted perfectly with the color of the taxi and if anyone noticed his black spots, they just assumed it was dirt from the city.

As the taxi rolled along the expressway, Bollo could hear the radio in the cab.

The announcer said, "Police were still searching this morning for Bollo, the million-dollar leopard, who escaped from Kennedy Airport last night. The Mayor has asked the public to remain calm. He also announced he had appointed a special commission to investigate the leopard problem in New York City.

"The Police Commissioner has ordered all leaves canceled until this dangerous man-eater is apprehended, and Felix the Furrier has offered a reward of twenty-five thousand dollars to anyone who captures Bollo dead or alive."

Bollo gulped, "Dead or alive."

The announcer continued, "Miss Lulu La Looche, the famous movie star, is so grief-stricken about the escape of her fur coat that she has indicated she might not attend the Oscar Awards dinner next month.

"Anyone having any information about

Bollo should call his local FBI office immediately. The leopard is armed and considered extremely dangerous."

Bollo said to no one in particular, "Who wouldn't be dangerous if they were going to skin him alive?"

The taxi crossed the Triborough Bridge, then drove down the East River Parkway, turned off at 63rd Street and deposited its passengers at the Plaza Hotel on Fifth Avenue.

Bollo did not know where he was, but he happened to see a park across from the Plaza and decided that would be the safest place to hide until night fell.

He dived off the taxi before it came to a stop and flew over the 59th Street wall into Central Park. Many people, of course, saw him, but, being New Yorkers, no one called the police because they didn't want to become involved.

Dashing through the park, Bollo found a clump of bushes to hide in.

He made himself as small as possible and waited for night to fall. Only once was he disturbed and that was when a man outside the clump of bushes said to an old lady, "This is a stick-up. Give me your pocketbook."

Bollo peered out the bushes to get a better look as to what was going on and when the man saw him, he screamed, dropped his gun, and ran off.

The old lady, who didn't know what frightened the thief, yelled after him, "Coward. Why don't you fight like a man?"

As soon as night fell, Bollo picked himself up and started looking for a way out of the park. He took a path that he thought would lead him to the street, but instead he walked right in to the Central Park Zoo. First he heard the elephants, then he heard the monkeys chattering and birds and finally the roar of the lion. Bollo leaped for joy. These were his people.

He ran into the lion's den. Since visiting hours were over, all the lions were surprised to see him.

"What are you doing here?" a lion said.

Bollo said, "I'm the man-eating leopard that everyone is searching for, but, frankly, I've never eaten a man. What does it taste like?"

"Chicken," an old lion said. "Say, you've

caused quite a storm in New York. Ever since you escaped, they've double-locked our cages and all leopards have been put in solitary confinement."

"I can't help that," Bollo said. "Listen, I'm in a spot. Do you have any good ideas for me?"

"You don't have a prayer," the old lion said. "You're as good as dead."

"But surely there must be some way to get out of this mess."

"I don't know of one," the lion said. "Unless—unless—"

"Unless what?"

"Unless you become an endangered species."

"What's an endangered species?"

"That means you're disappearing from the face of the earth and, therefore, it's against the law to kill you."

"I like that," Bollo said. "How do I become an endangered species?"

"I don't know," a lion replied. "But if you go in the Bear House, there's a polar bear who has been declared an endangered species and maybe he can tell you."

"Thanks," Bollo said and he left the Lion House and went over to the Bear House.

The polar bear was sleeping and was very annoyed when Bollo woke him up. "I ought to give you a clout on the head," the polar bear said, standing on his hind legs.

"Look, I'm sorry to bother you at this late hour, but I have a problem. How can I declare myself an endangered species?"

"You can't do it," the polar bear said with disgust in his voice. "It has to be done by an Act of Congress."

"What's Congress?"

"It's a bunch of men who sit around in Washington and decide what people can or cannot do in the country. If they pass a law that no one can kill you, then you're free as a bird. But I better warn you, they move awfully slow and by the time they got around to passing a law that you were an endangered species, you could be dead."

"How do I get to Washington?" Bollo asked.

"I'd recommend the Metroliner in this

kind of weather. It's a train that leaves every hour."

Before Bollo could thank the polar bear, he had gone back to sleep.

Bollo was given directions to Penn Station by a kangaroo. "Your best bet is to go into the open manhole on Seventh Avenue and 59th Street and follow the sewer down to 33rd Street. The sewer connects with a tunnel that leads directly to the trains. You'll see signs indicating which train is the Metroliner. Then hop on top and don't get off until the end of the line."

"I got you," Bollo said.

Bollo followed the directions and in less than an hour he was perched on the 7 A.M. Metroliner which was leaving for Washington, D.C.

The ride down was uneventful, and not very inspiring. Bollo could hardly breathe as the train rolled through smoggy New Jersey, smoggy Pennyslvania, smoggy Delaware, and smoggy Maryland. He thought to himself, "I wonder why people don't declare *themselves* an endangered species?"

While he catnapped on the top of the

train, he dreamed of his beloved Nefertiti and tears filled his eyes. Bollo longed to be at her side, but he knew it was not to be. Meanwhile events were taking place in the country that Bollo was not aware of.

A group of concerned citizens had formed a FREE BOLLO organization. A well-known musical conductor had held a cocktail party in his Park Avenue apartment the night before and had raised fifteen thousand dollars to pay for Bollo's legal bills. Jane Fonda and Marlon Brando had gone on the *Today Show* and attacked Felix the Furrier and Lulu La Looche for wanting to make Bollo into a fur coat.

To counteract them The Leopard Furriers of America got together a war fund to protect their right to make fur coats from any animals they wanted to.

The FBI was criticized because they couldn't find Bollo, and Lulu La Looche was still crying in her bed because she had lost her fur coat.

As the Metroliner came into Union Station in Washington, D.C., Bollo tried to figure his next move. He didn't know where Congress was, and even if he found it, he knew it would be impossible to explain to anyone that he wanted to be declared an endangered species. He decided to get off in the railroad yards in case there were any police waiting for him in the station.

Just before the Metroliner came to a halt, Bollo hopped off and ran to a siding. No one was in sight and he made a beeline across the tracks. But he found himself blocked by a large train with bars on it.

Bollo crawled underneath the train, but when he got to the other side, he saw twelve trucks with giant cages on them. A man with a whip was screaming with a heavy accent, "Effrybody in the cages. Effrybody in the cages." Bollo froze.

The man with the whip saw Bollo. "You dere, in de cage. Vat are you doing under the train? Hurry up or I giff you a good kick in the behind."

The situation struck Bollo as so ridiculous he wanted to laugh. But he thought better of it. Besides there were several large pieces of horse meat in the cage and by now hunger had got the better of him.

"Hokay, boy," said the man with the whip. "Dis is my last varning."

Bollo jumped into the cage and dived for the horse meat. He found himself fighting with a tiger over it.

"Enuff," said the man swinging his whip at both the tiger and Bollo. "I throw cold vater on both of you if you don't stop mit the fighting."

The tiger backed away and eyed Bollo warily. Bollo kept one paw on the horse meat but was prepared to defend himself.

"What are you doing in my cage?" the tiger said.

"He told me to get in," Bollo said.

"But you're not part of the circus."

"Is that what this thing is?" Bollo said in amazement.

"Yes, we're part of the circus and we're going to play two weeks at the Coliseum."

"Well, I'll be a monkey's uncle," said Bollo. "Whoever thought I'd wind up in a circus."

"You still haven't explained what you're doing with my horse meat," the tiger said menacingly.

"Don't get in an uproar," Bollo said. "I came to Washington to have myself declared an endangered species and as I was crossing the tracks that guy with a whip told me to get into the cage, and I figured I had better or someone was going to shoot me and make me into a fur coat."

"Are you crazy or something?" the tiger asked.

"Here's your horse meat," said Bollo wearily. "I'll explain the whole thing."

As the truck made its way toward the Coliseum, Bollo told the tiger his sad story.

"Wow, I've heard some wild animal stories in my time," the tiger said, "but this takes the cake."

"What do you think I ought to do now?"

"You'd better stay with us for a while until things cool off."

"But how?" Bollo said. "As soon as we get to the Coliseum, they'll discover I don't belong to the circus and they'll call the police."

"Don't worry about that. You know the man with the whip? He's called Torga the Absent-minded Animal Trainer. He can't remember *anything.* He probably thinks you belong to his act. Stick with us tigers when we get to the Coliseum and he'll assume you're one of us."

"But, I'm a *leopard*," Bollo protested.

"He didn't notice the difference when he told you to get into the cage, did he?"

"No," Bollo agreed, "but I've never been in a circus. I wouldn't know what to do."

"You do what Torga tells you. When he says dance on the box, dance on the box. When he tells you to jump over a tiger, jump over a tiger; when he says roll over on your back, you roll on your back. A child could do it. The one thing to remember is to growl a lot. Torga wants the audience to think we're ferocious."

"Do you think the other tigers will mind if I join the act?"

"It doesn't make any difference to them. One more animal in the cage will give them less work to do. Here, have a piece of horse meat."

"I'll never forget this, tiger," Bollo said.

"My name is Exxon, like in the gasoline."

The trucks arrived at the Coliseum and Bollo and Exxon were unloaded into a large cage in the animal tent. Exxon introduced Bollo to the other tigers and, when he told them what had happened, they roared with laughter. "That dumb animal trainer," one of the tigers said. "He can't tell a horse from a rabbit. He's lucky we haven't eaten him alive."

"I want you to understand, tigers," said Bollo, "that as soon as I make my petition to Congress to be declared an endangered species, I won't bother you anymore."

"It's no skin off our backs," a tiger said.

Bollo had a pained look on his face.

"Sorry about that," the tiger said.

"My problem is that I don't know how to go about getting Congress to pass a law to declare me an endangered species."

"Why don't you talk to Edgar the Elephant? He's been coming to Washington for twenty years with the circus. He should know."

Exxon called over to Edgar, who was right next to the cage munching on a ton of dandelion greens.

"Edgar, we have something to ask you."

"Not while I'm eating," Edgar said.

"This is important. We have an escaped leopard with us and they are going to kill him and make him into a fur coat unless he can get Congress to pass a law declaring him an endangered species. How can he get a law passed?"

Edgar the Elephant scratched his head with his trunk. "It's not easy. Of course, if you were a voter—but animals don't have the right to vote so Congress really isn't that interested in the problem."

"But if I just simply stated our case," Bollo said.

"You've got a lot to learn. Congress will only move if someone pressures them. You have to lobby for a law."

"Lobby?"

"Yes, you know, visit the lawmakers in their offices and stop them in the hallways and say, 'How about voting for my bill?'"

"I can't do that," Bollo said. "They'd never listen to a leopard."

"I guess you're right," Edgar replied. "We're going to have to give this some serious thought. It's an interesting case and I might take it without charging you a fee."

"He's smart," Exxon assured Bollo. "He'll come up with a solution."

While Bollo was safely quartered at the Coliseum with his new-found tiger friends, the search for him was extended all along the eastern seaboard.

A picture of Bollo's head, supplied by Felix the Furrier, was posted in every police station and Bollo was put on the "Ten Most Wanted" animal list.

Housewives were warned to lock their doors and not to let any strange-looking cats into their houses. Armed posse patrolled the streets of the cities at night. Because of the large reward offered by Felix, people reported they saw Bollo in Columbus, Ohio; Bangor, Maine; Springfield, Illinois, and as far away as Jumping Jack, Arizona.

Of course, all the information was wrong because Bollo was in Washington, D.C.

The next few days were glorious ones for Bollo. As part of Torga's Tiger Act, Bollo did two shows a day—one in the afternoon

and one in the evening. As Exxon predicted, there really was nothing to being a trained tiger in a circus. All you had to do was jump up, sit down, roll over, and look ferocious. Torga snapped his whip a lot, but he never used it on the tigers, except once in a while to hit them on the nose when they were sluggish.

The most interesting thing was that the act got more applause in Washington than anywhere. Torga couldn't understand it. But the truth is the audience had never seen a leopard doing tricks with tigers before.

After the evening show, Bollo and Edgar talked about Bollo's problem.

"I've been giving a great deal of thought to this," Edgar said. "We're going to have to work real fast because when Torga gets his horse meat bill at the end of the week, he's going to realize he's got one tiger too many in his act."

"Maybe he'll let me stay on?" Bollo suggested.

"He can't, even if he wanted to. Legally you belong to Felix the Furrier or Lulu La Looche. Now, as I see it, Congress won't want to pass a law for one leopard. But if we could get you in an omnibus bill with a lot of other endangered species, I think we could pull if off."

"An omnibus bill?" Bollo said.

"Yes, a bill which would include all sorts of animals—grizzly bears, antelopes, whooping cranes, bald eagles, giant pandas, mountain gorillas, American buffalo, and white-throated wallabys—any animal that's being threatened with extinction. If it covered many animals, it's quite possible Congress would pass a law."

"That's great. How do we do it?"

"Well, you know Franco in the Brothers Four that do the motorcycle act?"

"You mean the four French poodles?"

"Right. Franco has been trained to write in English. He could draft a document that you could deliver to Congress and which would be read by a Senator who would then introduce a bill."

"That's wonderful," Bollo said. "What should we say?"

"We have to give it a lot of thought because this could be a very important document which could affect all animals for years to come," Edgar said.

A committee was set up consisting of Bollo, Edgar the Elephant, Franco the French poodle, and Sarah the trained seal. Ideas were brought up and rejected. Other animals submitted proposals. There were debates late into the night. Some got so lively that the clowns complained to Torga they couldn't get any sleep.

After three days, Edgar dictated the final document to Franco, who wrote it down on the outside of a large brown shopping bag that the horse meat had come in.

It read, "We, the animals of the world, petition Congress to pass a law declaring all wild species of the earth as endangered species. We ask you to save our hides, preserve our feathers, and protect our fins from the two-legged species called man.

"We do not wish to become fur coats, handbags, ladies' hats, piano keys, ashtrays, belts, shoes, car robes, wall mountings, or rugs for the fireplace. We want to live out our lives in the jungles, the forests, the mountains, the rivers, and the seas. We beg you,

We, the animals of the world...

in your wisdom, to protect us from the stupidity of human beings who walk the earth searching us out with guns, nets and traps for their own selfish reasons. Amen."

Everyone agreed the document was brilliant. "Bollo," said Edgar, "if you get a law passed, you will be doing a great service for every animal in the world."

As they were talking, they heard sirens outside the tent. Everyone's ears went up.

A man's voice said, "We hear there's a leopard in the tiger act."

"Impossible," Torga shouted. "I haff no leopards mitt the tigers."

"We're looking for Bollo the leopard, and one of our informers told us he was hiding out in the circus."

"Sauerkraut," Torga said. "You don't think I know a leopard from a tiger?"

Edgar said, "You better get out of here, Bollo."

"I can't jump over the cage. The bars are too high."

"Wait," said Exxon. "We'll make a pyramid and you can climb on top of us."

Four tigers stood on the bottom, three

tigers jumped on them, two tigers on top of them, and Exxon was the last on. Bollo put the brown shopping bag in his mouth and leaped up on top of the tigers and vaulted over the cage, landing in sawdust on the other side. Edgar lifted up the back part of the tent with his trunk and Bollo dashed out, just as Torga and four policemen came in the other side.

"You see. Is nothing but tigers in the cage," Torga said.

The policemen aimed their flashlights all over the tent.

"I guess it must have been a mistake," one of them said.

Torga roared with laughter. "Imagine me haffing a leopard in my tiger act."

The tigers rolled over on their backs; they could hardly contain themselves.

Since it was night, Bollo could see the lights of the Capitol off in the distance and, taking the darkest streets, he made his way toward them. He arrived just at dawn, and while they were raising the flag over the Capitol, all the guards around the building stood at strict attention with their eyes on the Stars and Stripes. Bollo darted up into the Capitol and ran through the empty halls looking for a place to hide. He saw a large sign which said SENATE and pushed the swinging door open. There were one hundred desks on the floor and a large desk up on a platform at the head of the room.

He went up there and looked around. There was an opening underneath the desk with a large wastepaper basket sitting there. Bollo crawled into this wastepaper basket and waited.

It was a long wait because the Senate does not meet until noon. When the bell finally rang, Bollo was prepared to deliver his petition. But there was no one on the Senate floor except one Senator droning along about a dam in North Dakota. Bollo decided to bide his time. At two o'clock, a vote

was called and the Senators started to come in. As soon as he saw he had a quorum—enough Senators to vote—Bollo leaped out of the wastepaper basket up on the desk and placed the brown paper bag on the head of the Presiding Officer of the Senate, who happened to be the Vice President of the United States. The women in the galleries screamed. The Vice President jumped off the platform and all the Senators dived under their desks.

"Get the police!" someone shouted.

"Call out the Marines!" another Senator screamed.

"Where is the Air Force?"

Armed guards appeared in the galleries.

"Don't shoot!" someone yelled. "You could hit a Senator."

It was becoming obvious to Bollo that no one wanted to read his petition so he dropped it on the floor and decided to get out of there fast. Bollo climbed up to the Press Gallery, then dashed through the hall, down the two flights of steps, and out into broad daylight with police in hot pursuit.

He started running up Pennsylvania Avenue. He ran between the automobiles, past the FBI building, the Post Office, and the City Hall. An air raid siren had gone off, and people were running in all directions.

Off ahead Bollo saw a large white building with a fence around it. It had lots of bushes and a gigantic green lawn. Bollo leaped over the fence and started across the lawn.

It was Bollo's worst mistake. For there on the lawn were members of the U. S. Army, U. S. Air Force, U. S. Navy, and U. S. Marines all neatly lined up for a parade. And just a few feet away from them, standing with his wife, was the President of the United States. Of all places to hide, Bollo had chosen the White House, the most heavily guarded home in America.

A secret serviceman spied Bollo and drew his gun. Two more secret servicemen drew their guns. The U.S. soldiers, sailors, and marines brought their rifles to their shoulders, ready to fire.

Bollo had no way out. He decided to roll over on his back as he had done in the circus.

The President said, "Don't shoot him."

Those were exactly the words Bollo wanted to hear.

"Tie him up and get him out of here," the President said. "I don't want to ruin the Emperor's state visit."

What Bollo had gotten himself into was this. Everyone was standing on the White House lawn awaiting the arrival of the Emperor of Ethiopia, also known as the "Lion of Judah," who was paying a state visit to the United States. The Emperor was being brought to the White House by the President's private helicopter. As the President does with all heads of state, he had arranged for a ceremony on the lawn with members of the Armed Forces and U. S. Marine Corps Band. This is a very important ceremony and it wouldn't look very good for the President of the United States to greet the Emperor of Ethiopia with a dead leopard on the lawn.

As two secret servicemen tied up Bollo's feet, the roar of the helicopter could be heard overhead. The Emperor of Ethiopia was about to land and it was too late to get Bollo off the grass. So the two secret servicemen held him by the ropes they had tied to his legs. He was quite uncomfortable in this position, but still very much alive.

The helicopter landed on the pad and out stepped the Emperor, a magnificent man in a uniform of red and black velvet with gold stripes down his pants. He shook hands with the President. The President shook hands with him. He shook hands with the President's wife; the President's wife shook hands with him. The U. S. Marine Corps struck up the Ethiopian National Anthem. Then they played "The Star-Spangled Banner."

"Mr. President," the Emperor said over a microphone, "I am happy to be in your wonderful country and present you with this gift from my people, who hold you in such high esteem. It is the largest diamond in the world."

The President whispered to one of his aides, "What have we got to give him?"

The aide whispered back, "All we have is a ballpoint fountain pen with your name on it."

"We can't give him a fountain pen for the largest diamond in the world," the President said as the Emperor droned on about the great friendship between their countries.

The President's wife, who overheard the conversation, whispered, "Why don't you give him the leopard?"

"Good thinking," the President whispered back to her.

The Emperor finally finished his speech

and the President began his. "Your Majesty, in the name of Ethiopian-American relations, I have the honor to present to you today, as a gift of the American people, this magnificent, beautiful, and rare leopard which I hope you will take back with you to your country."

The two secret servicemen half-dragged, half-lifted Bollo over to where the Emperor was standing.

The Emperor's eyes brimmed with tears. "It's just what I wanted. My pet leopard, Moses, died two days ago. How thoughtful of you, Mr. President."

"Think nothing of it, Your Majesty. I shall have him flown to your capital this morning in my private plane, *Air Force One*."

"That would be nice," the Emperor said. "Then I wouldn't have to carry him in my luggage."

The President nodded to the two secret servicemen, who carried Bollo, his legs still tied, over to the helicopter. In ten minutes the helicopter took off from the White House lawn and flew to Andrews Air Force Base,

where Bollo was transferred to the President's private plane, *Air Force One*. Bollo, who was now officially the pet leopard of the Emperor of Ethiopia, was given royal treatment. He was placed in an enormous box filled with foam rubber. In the box were ten pounds of hamburger and three gallons of milk. And just so Bollo wouldn't get bored during the flight, they showed him the movie *Born Free*.

Meanwhile, back at the Senate Chambers, a furious floor debate was going on.

Senator Blimpbutter said, "I demand that Bollo the leopard be held in contempt of Congress."

Senator Nickelsworth said, "I move that all animals be banned from within three blocks of the Capitol."

Senator Calloweather said, "Never in the history of this illustrious Congress have I witnessed a more un-American display of conduct. I propose we have a Congressional investigation to find out how this leopard got into the Senate and I move we appropriate one million dollars to see that it doesn't happen again."

But one silver-maned Senator, whose name was Washbutton, got on his feet and said, "Gentlemen, we are missing the point. We have not asked ourselves what an African leopard was doing in Washington, D.C. Did he fly here? Did he swim here? Did he walk here? No, gentlemen, he was brought here in a cage. And why was he brought here in a cage? To make a fur coat for a Hollywood movie star.

"Is it not time we stopped this useless slaughter of rare animals throughout the world? How long can we go on killing the beautiful beasts whose only crime is that they have desirable skin that can be made into fur coats and trophies.

"We have it in our power to declare these animals endangered species and to give them full protection under the law. Let us not allow this moment to go by because a leopard crashed into our hallowed halls. Let us use this opportunity to show the world that America will no longer stand idly by and see the wildlife of the globe destroyed, never to walk the earth again."

Many Senators were crying, as were all the tourists in the gallery.

"Gentlemen, I propose an omnibus bill, protecting all endangered species from destruction."

"Where is your bill?" the Vice President said.

"Here it is," Senator Washbutton said. And he handed the Vice President the brown shopping bag he had found on the floor under his desk.

The Vice President hit his gavel. "All those in favor say aye."

One hundred Senators yelled, "Aye."

"All those opposed say nay."

There was dead silence in the Senate.

"So be it," the Vice President said. "The ayes have it and your bill has been passed unanimously."

Reporters noted it was the first thing the Senate had been able to agree on in twenty years.

Meanwhile, back at the White House, the President was in his Oval Office after finishing a formal luncheon with the Emperor of Ethiopia.

"That was a close call with the gift for

the Emperor," the President said to his aide. "He seemed very pleased with the animal."

The President's aide said, "Felix the Furrier has been trying to call you all morning. He saw you on television give away his Somali leopard to the Emperor of Ethiopia and he's furious."

"I'll take care of him," the President said. "Get me Felix the Furrier on the phone."

The aide, after dialing the number, gave the President the phone. The President spoke. "Felix, this is the President of the United States. I want to thank you personally for the gift you provided us with for the Emperor of Ethiopia."

"Gift?" Felix croaked.

"Yes. The Emperor was terribly pleased. You are a great American, Felix, for what you have done, and your name will go down in the history books. I am having a postage stamp made up in your honor."

"A postage stamp?" Felix the Furrier stammered.

"Yes. I could do no less."

"But what about Lulu La Looche's fur coat?" Felix said.

"I will call Lulu La Looche personally," the President said.

The President telephoned Lulu La Looche. "Lulu, this is the President of the United States. Would you like to come to the White House for dinner next week?"

"Of course, dahling," said Lulu. "I thought you'd nevaire ask."

"Good, but don't wear a fur coat," the President said. "My wife has only a cloth coat and she would feel terrible if anyone wore a fur to our dinner."

"Dahling," said Lulu La Looche, "I hate fur coats. I wouldn't be caught dead in one."

While you are reading this, Bollo is now back at the palace in Ethiopia and is the Emperor's favorite pet. The first thing he did when he returned was seek out his beloved Nefertiti, whom he never thought he would see again.

Nefertiti was so happy to see Bollo that she licked him all over for joy. That night as they both lay on the banana leaves, Bollo asked Nefertiti to marry him. Nefertiti said, "Yes," and they now have three cubs named Edgar, Exxon, and Nixxon.

The Emperor of Ethiopia was so pleased when Nefertiti gave birth that he had a special tree house built for Bollo's family. This is where Bollo lives when he isn't entertaining important visitors at the palace.

Bollo has become a legend in Africa and all the rare animals know they owe him a debt of gratitude for saving their lives.

Despite his notoriety, Bollo is still the same modest cat he always was. "All I did was convince the Americans that the only one who has a right to wear a leopard fur coat is a leopard."